Published in 2004 by Mercury Books London
20 Bloomsbury Street, London WC1B 3JH

© text copyright Enid Blyton Limited
© copyright original illustrations, Hodder and Stoughton Limited
© new illustrations 2004 Mercury Books London

Designed and produced for Mercury Books
by Open Door Limited, Langham, Rutland

Title: The Beautiful Cricket Ball & The Little Toy Stove
ISBN: 1 904668 31 3

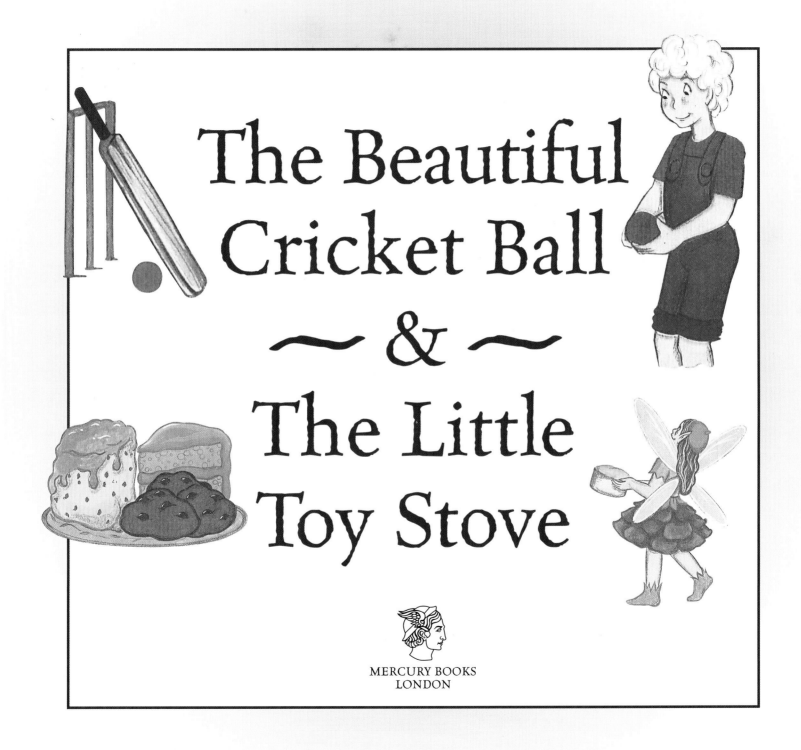

The Beautiful Cricket Ball

~ & ~

The Little Toy Stove

MERCURY BOOKS
LONDON

The Beautiful Cricket Ball

The boys were going to play cricket. There were the twins, Peter and John, Alec, Tom, Jim, Fred, Ian, and Hugh. What fun it would be!

"We will play on that nice smooth stretch of sand!" said Peter. "You put the stumps in, John!"

Little Harry came running up. "Peter, Peter!" he cried. "Can I play too?"

"No," said Peter.
"You're too small."

"But I can run fast," said Harry. "Oh, do let me play, Peter. I won't ask to bat – just let me field for you."

"No, we've got enough players," said Peter.
"Run along and play with your sister, Harry."

Harry was very disappointed.
He had so hoped to play cricket
with the big boys. It would have
been such fun. He could run
very fast and, although he didn't
bat very well, he could bowl quite
straight. He went off, hurt and
sad. Peter might have given him
a chance!

His little sister was building
a castle. "Come and help,
Harry," she said.

Harry took
up his spade
and began
to dig. It
was no good
being horrid
to Susan
just because
someone had
been horrid
to him!

The boys drove in the stumps – and then Fred brought out a most beautiful new cricket ball.

"Look, boys," he said. "Here's a fine ball! I had it for my birthday yesterday!"

"My!" said Peter and the others, looking at the beautiful ball admiringly. "That's a beauty! Can we play with it to-day, Fred?"

"Yes," said Fred, proudly. "But will you let me bat first if I let you play with my new ball?"

"All right," said the others. "Take the bat, Fred. Who's going to bowl? You, John! See if you can get Fred out with his own ball?"

The game began. Harry, still digging castles, could hear the click of the ball against the bat as Fred drove it over the sand and then ran.

The boys shouted. They ran after the ball and threw it in. John stopped bowling and Ian began. It all looked very jolly indeed, and Harry wished and wished he could have played too.

At last Fred was bowled out. He gave up the bat to Peter, who was a very good batsman indeed. Hugh took the fine new ball to bowl to Peter. It felt so good as he twirled it about – the best ball the boys had ever had to play with!

Hugh bowled, and Peter struck out. The ball flew along the sand, and Peter ran, and ran and ran. He meant to make more runs than anyone else that morning! At last the ball was thrown in again and Hugh caught it. He bowled it to Peter again. Peter slashed out with the bat. Click! Went the ball. The ball flew towards the rocks.

"Stop it, Ian, stop it!" yelled Fred. "Don't let it go among the rocks, or we shall lose it."

But Ian could not stop it, for the ball was going too fast. It rolled fast towards the rocks. It struck once and flew up into the air – then it dropped somewhere.

"Find it, find it, Ian!" yelled everyone.

"Hurry! Peter is making more runs than anyone!"

Ian hunted round the rocks. He could not see the ball anywhere. How he hunted! He looked under the seaweed. He looked in every pool. That beautiful new ball was not to be seen!

At last the others came to help him look too. They peered here and there, they splashed into the pools, but it wasn't a bit of good – that ball could not be found!

"It's gone," said Fred, very much upset. "Quite disappeared. What shall we do?"

"Better play with our old one," said John. So the old one was got out and the game went on. But everyone was very sad about Fred's fine new ball. It was too bad to lose it the very first game.

Harry had been digging all the time the boys were hunting for the ball. He didn't like to go near them, for he was afraid they would send him away again. He did not know whether they had found the ball or not – but when he saw them playing again he thought they must have found their ball. He didn't know it was the old one.

The castle was finished at last. Susan wanted to do something else. "Let's go shrimping," she said.

"All right," said Harry.
"We'll catch some shrimps
for your tea, Susan."

They took their shrimping nets and went to the rockpools. They pushed their nets through the sand and looked to see how many shrimps they had caught.

"Only one tiny crab," said Susan, and she and Harry put their nets in the water again.

"I can see a big prawn!" suddenly shouted Harry, in delight. "Hurrah! Come here into my net, prawn!"

But the prawn would not be caught. He darted here and there, and at last disappeared under a shelving rock that jutted out into the pool. Harry stuck his net under the rock to catch the prawn.

He drew his net out and looked into it –
no – there was no prawn there!

"Harry, something rolled out from under
that rock when you stuck your net there,"
said Susan, pointing. "What was it?"

Harry looked down into the pool. He saw
a big red ball there. He picked it up. "It must
have been under that ledge of rock," he said.
"And when I poked my net underneath it
must have made the ball roll out. I wonder
whose ball it is."

"It belongs to those boys," said Susan. "I heard them say they hadn't found their ball. They are playing with another one."

"Are they really, Susan?" said Harry. "This must be Fred's beautiful new ball then. He must have been upset when it couldn't be found."

"Are you going to take
it back to them?"
asked Susan.

"I don't know,"
said Harry.
"They were horrid to me this morning.
I don't see why I should be nice to them."

"But Fred will be so sad if he doesn't get his
new ball back," said kind-hearted Susan.
"Don't you remember how bad we felt when
we lost our new kite, Harry?"

 "Yes," said Harry. "All right, I'll take it back to the boys."

He dried the ball on a towel, and then ran to where the boys were playing. He waited until the batsman was bowled out and then yelled to Peter:

"Peter! I've found Fred's new ball! It was in the rock-pool, catch!"

The boys turned in surprise. Fred gave a cheer. "Hurrah! I'm so glad!"

Peter caught the ball and stared at Harry. "That's jolly good of you," he said. "You are a sport! I say, boys, what about letting him come into the game? He must be a good sort to bring back our ball when we wouldn't let him play this morning!"

"Yes, let him come!" roared all the boys. "Come on, young Harry! We'll let you play with us. It was decent of you to give back our ball!"

So Harry joined the game – and wasn't
he pleased and proud. He fields very well
indeed and, do you know, although he only
made one run, he bowled out Ian and Hugh.
The boys were quite surprised.

"You play a good game, Harry," said Peter, at the end. "You can come and play with us again to-morrow."

Now Harry always plays cricket with the big boys

– and how glad he is that he took Susan's advice and was nice to the boys when he really didn't want to be!

28

As for Fred's beautiful new ball, they are still playing with it. Its stay in the rock-pool didn't hurt it a bit!

The Little Toy Stove

Angela had a little toy stove. It was a dear little stove, with an oven that had two doors, and three rings at the top to put kettles or saucepans on. At the back was a shelf to warm plates or keep the dinner hot. Angela liked it very much.

But Mother wouldn't let her cook anything on her stove. "No, Angela," she said, "you are not big enough. I am afraid you would burn yourself if you lighted the stove and tried to cook something."

"Oh, but Mother, it isn't any fun unless I can cook myself something!" said Angela, nearly crying. But Mother wouldn't let her light the stove, so it was no use saying any more.

Now one day, as Angela was playing with her saucepans and kettles in the garden, filling them with bits of grass for vegetables, and

little berries for potatoes and apples,
pretending to cook them all for dinner,
she heard a tiny voice calling to her.

"Angela! Angela! Do you think you would mind lending me your stove for this evening? My stove has gone wrong, and I have a party. I simply must cook for my guests, and so I wondered if you'd lend me your stove!"

Angela looked all round to see who was speaking. At last she saw a tiny elf, not more than six inches high, peeping at her from behind a flower.

"Oh!" said Angela in delight. "I've never seen a fairy before. Do come and let me look at you."

The elf ran out from behind the flower. She was dressed in blue and silver, and had long shining wings and a tiny pointed face. Angela thought she was lovely.

"Will you lend me your stove?" asked the elf. "Please say yes."

"Of course!" said Angela. "I'd love to. Will you really cook on it? My mother won't let me."

"Of course she won't let you," said the elf. "You aren't big enough yet. You might burn yourself."

"Shall I leave my stove here for you?" asked Angela.

"Yes, please," said the elf. "I can easily cook out here. It is to be an open-air party. I live behind those hollyhocks, so I shan't have far to bring my things."

"I suppose I couldn't come and watch you?" said Angela longingly. "I've never seen my toy stove really doing cooking, you know!"

"Well, you come and watch to-night," said the elf. "I shall begin my cooking at nine o'clock. The party begins at eleven."

Angela was so excited when she went in to bed. She meant to put on her dressing-gown and get up at nine o'clock, and creep down the garden.

So she lay awake until she heard the hall clock chime nine. Then up she got and slipped down the stairs and out of the garden door.

She could quite well see where her toy stove was, because smoke was rising from it.
The elf had got it going well. A lovely smell of baking and roasting came on the air. Oooh!

You should have seen the elf cooking on that stove. The oven was full of things roasting away well. The plates were getting nice and hot in the plate-rack!

"Just listen to my pudding boiling away in that saucepan," said the elf, pleased. "This stove cooks very well indeed; it's a fine stove."

"What sort of pudding is it?" asked Angela.

"It's a tippy-top pudding," said the elf. "And I'm cooking a poppity cake too and some google buns."

"Oh my, they do sound delicious," said Angela, "and so exciting! I've never heard of them before. I suppose I couldn't come to the party?"

"No," said the elf. "It is too late a party for little girls like you. But, Angela, as I think it is really very kind of you to let me use your lovely stove for my cooking, I'd like you to taste some of my dishes. Listen!

There is sure to be some tippy-top pudding, some poppity cake, and a few google buns over after the party. If there are I will put them on a plate and leave them inside the oven. See?

I will clean the stove nicely, too, and leave it all shiny and bright. Now, good night, dear. You must go to bed. You are yawning."

"Good night!" said Angela, and she ran off. In the morning she went to see if there was anything inside her oven. And what do you think? There was a neat little blue dish, and on one side of it was a slice of yellow tippy-top pudding, and on the other side were three google buns, red and blue, and a large slice of green poppity cake! Ooooh!

Angela ate them all – and they were simply delicious. She does so hope the elf will want to borrow her stove again. Wouldn't it be lovely if she did?

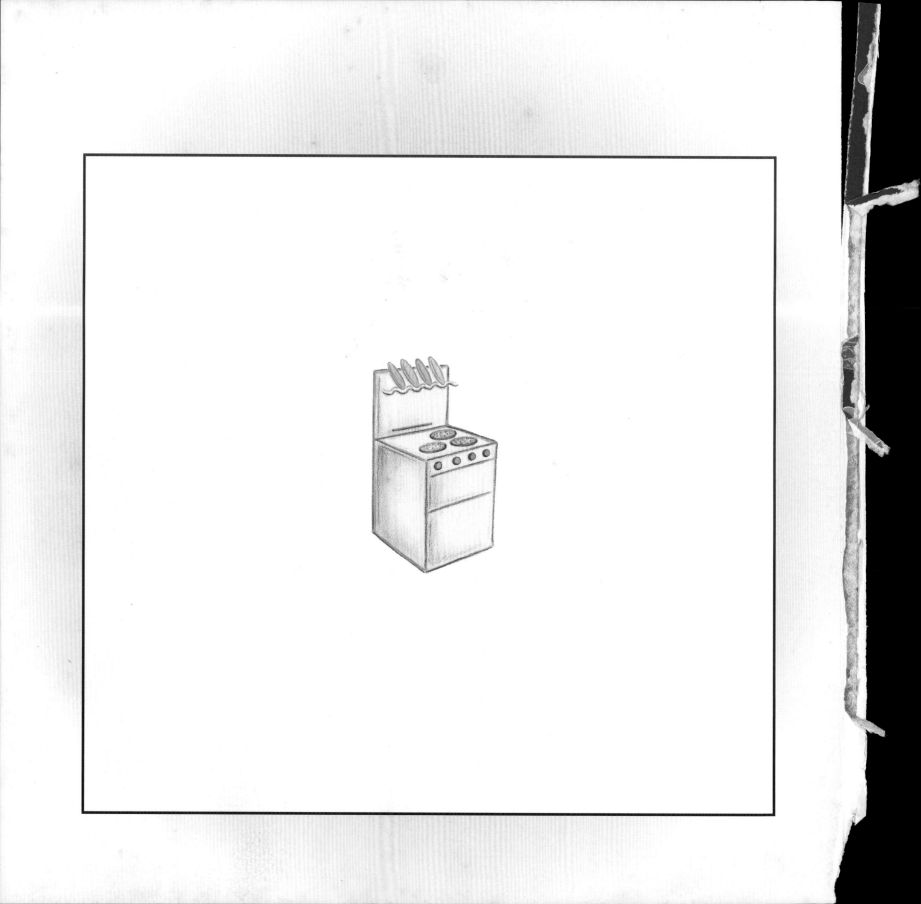

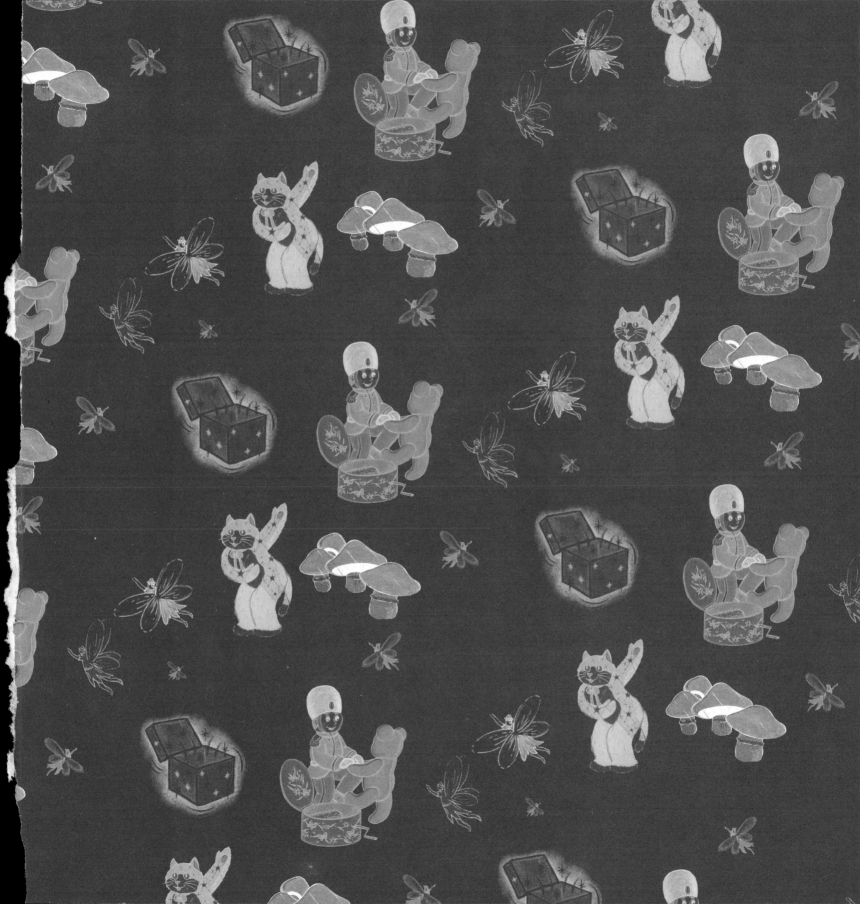